How to DRAW

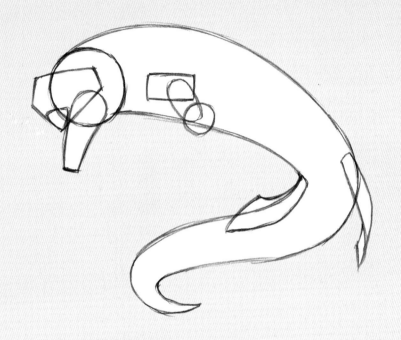

BIG, BAD
BIBLE BEASTS

WRITTEN AND ILLUSTRATED BY ROYDEN LEPP

How to DRAW

BIG, BAD
BIBLE BEASTS

WRITTEN AND ILLUSTRATED BY ROYDEN LEPP

zonder**kidz**

ZONDERVAN.COM/
AUTHOR**TRACKER**

zonderkidz
The children's group of Zondervan

www.zonderkidz.com

How to Draw Big, Bad Bible Beasts
Copyright © 2007 by Royden Lepp
Illustrations © 2007 by Royden Lepp

Requests for information should be addressed to:
Grand Rapids, Michigan 49530

Library of Congress Cataloging-in-Publication Data

Lepp, Royden, 1980-
    How to draw good, bad & ugly Bible beasts /
  by Royden Lepp.
      p. cm.
     ISBN-13: 978-0-310-71336-4 (softcover)
     ISBN-10: 0-310-71336-6 (softcover)
  1. Animals in art–Juvenile literature. 2. Drawing Technique–Juvenile literature. 3. Animals in the
Bible–Juvenile literature. 4. Bible–Illustrations–Juvenile literature. I. Title.
NC780.L36 2007
743.6–dc22
                                         2006020358

Editor: Bruce Nuffer
Art direction and design: Laura Maitner-Mason

Printed in China

07 08 09 10 11 • 10 9 8 7 6 5 4 3 2 1

Table of Contents

Hi! My name is Royden. I've been drawing my whole life. When I was young I tried to draw at least once a day. Now I'm drawing every day before my job, for my job, and when I get home from work.

What I've found is that drawing isn't easy and it takes a lot of practice. This book of lessons will teach you to duplicate some drawings I've done. In the process I hope you will learn a few things about technique. Don't get discouraged if your drawings don't look just like mine. It will take several tries before you get something you're happy with. A good artist must be patient and hardworking.

But if you find that these drawings were easy, remember not to brag, because it was God who gave you the ability to draw. Thank God every day for the talents he's given you. Your drawing is the same as singing songs in church—it's a form of worship to God—so draw as much as you can! And have fun!!

Instruction

Making a good drawing is like building a house. So make sure you have all the right tools. You're going to need a couple pencils, a pencil sharpener, a pen, and an eraser.

We start these drawings by making basic geometric shapes. Make sure you keep these light and rough. The lines don't have to be clean or dark at all. We'll keep adding shapes in each step until the "foundation" of the drawing is complete. Then about halfway through the lesson we'll switch to either a pen or a darker pencil with a softer lead to build the detail. At that step you should erase the basic shapes a little. Ask your parents for help if you want.

Notice the little pencil and pen symbols by the drawings. These indicate whether you are using pencil for sketching or pen for outlining and adding detail.

After each lesson a detail section focuses on a specific part of the drawing.

Once you've finished a drawing, you may send it to me for feedback. Scan it and send it to royden.lepp@gmail.com and I'll post it on this website: www.roydenshowtodraw. blogspot.com/ Go to this website to see my comments on your drawings and the drawings of other kids.

All right! Let's grab our tools and draw!

Horse ①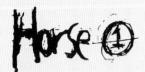

I think it's safe to say that in Bible times, horses were used a lot for war. Can you imagine if you were standing on the battlefield, and suddenly a cavalry of armored warriors rode in from the right or from the left? What a scary thought! If you found yourself in a battle in the Old Testament, you would want to be up on a horse instead of on your own two feet. The horse we're going to draw is outfitted for Old Testament battle. There were no saddles in those days. There was no horse armor besides maybe some leather coverings. All right...let's draw!

Step ①

Well, this is a pretty easy start. Notice the sizes and positions of the three circles.

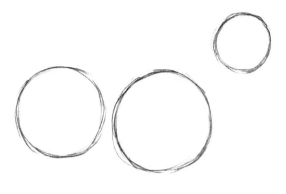

Step ②

Okay, this looks a little more like a horse. Because one of the back legs is hidden by the tail, we're going to just focus on three right now.

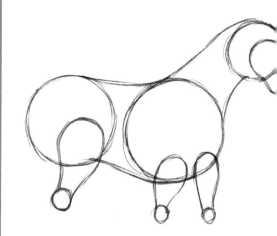

Step ③

There are lots of circles and tubes in the legs and tail. Try to keep your eye on all the proportions and shapes. Add the ears and the line of the mane.

Step ④

Now you have the basic shapes—the framework—needed to build this complex drawing. Add the saddle blanket, hooves, and chest harness.

Use a pen to outline the horse. Add the face, mane, and reins. Try to copy the bumpy lines on the tail and legs as much as you can, because you'll need them later.

Draw lines to start the woven tail. Add the bridle and muscle detail. Look at pictures of a real bridle if it helps. Start erasing pencil lines.

Now we're adding all the cloth around the legs as well as the leather covering across the lower neck. Finish the detail in the mane.

Lastly, add the final cross-weaving in the tail, the little studs on the leather covering, and the tassels on the blanket. There's also a strap with a buckle going underneath the belly. Good job! This kind of sketching takes time and patience.

Head Detail ①

The more you practice these drawings, the better you'll get, so don't get discouraged if this horse didn't turn out exactly how you thought it should. Let's look more closely at the head. The head is very complicated. See if these few extra steps iron out some problems.

 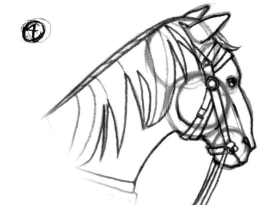

Horse ②

Horses were a very important mode of transportation in Bible times. Since they're such amazing creatures, we're going to draw one from a different perspective. The trickiest part of drawing horses is their legs, with their many joints and tendons. Print out some pictures of horses to look at while you're drawing this one. Maybe you'll notice some things that I didn't about those knobby knees.

Step ①

We're going to connect these circles together to build the body of the horse. Keep your pencil lines light and sketchy.

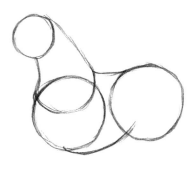

Step ②

The legs and head are developing. Notice how some of these shapes are not what they seem. The back leg starts with an oval.

Step ③

The legs are made up of lots of circles and tubes. Take your time to get those crazy angles right. Notice the pentagon on the face.

Step ④

Here are the hooves, the mane, and the tail. Now we're ready to switch to pen or dark pencil and lightly erase those simple shapes.

Step ⑤

The key to making this outline work is to look to the final image and notice where the detail is going to be. Try to keep all the curves and bumps in the lines.

Step ⑥

The eyes, ear detail, and the nostril are all you need to add next. If you're struggling with the head, just look at the detail section.

Step ⑦

Add long lines to the tail. Also add some very small detail around the hooves and on the head. They're just little lines but they're important.

Step ⑧

Finally, add lines to the mane, as well as musculature to the legs and body. This was a hard drawing for me. You may need to try it two or three times. Every time you do it, you will get better. I promise!

Head Detail ②

This horse head has a perspective and structure that makes it difficult to draw. Maybe if we break it down into all of its simple shapes, it will be easier to draw. Remember that these simple shapes represent everything under the surface that you can't see.

Lion ①

Lions are mentioned frequently in the Bible. One example is in the story of young David as a shepherd in his father's field. Samuel tells us that David used to fend off the lion with nothing but a sling and a club. Next time you're at the zoo, imagine young David in there saying, "Bring it on lion! I can take you with God on my side!" Sound familiar? He said similar things to that Philistine giant, Goliath.

Step ①

As you draw these simple shapes, keep the size and position in perspective.

 # Step ②

We're going to add these vase shapes to build the powerful legs. Also, add shapes to define the face and connect the body parts. Keep your pencil lines light.

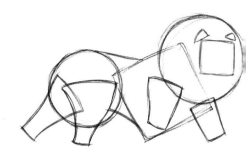

 # Step ③

We're adding more shapes here on the legs and the face.

 # Step ④

Now add rectangles to the legs to define the paws. Add the tail and eyes.
We're ready to start the final outline with pen and erase some pencil sketches.

Look to the final drawing as you outline the legs and face. The mane is less complicated because you started with a big circle. Don't let all that line work intimidate you: your drawing doesn't have to look exactly like mine.

Lions have an intense gaze. To get a better image of lions' eyes, look at some photos in books or on nature websites.

All we added here were some lines along the belly and legs to describe the muscle and strength of this big cat.

What else are we missing? Claws of course! I'm sure David didn't miss those claws. Make sure that all of the original shapes are erased. (But if they're not, it's okay. I always like a drawing where I can see the construction lines a little bit.)

Tail Detail

For this detail section, we're going to look at the tail. It will give you an idea of how I break up hair and fur. You can use these tricks on the mane and the legs as well. Feel free to color your drawing when you're finished.

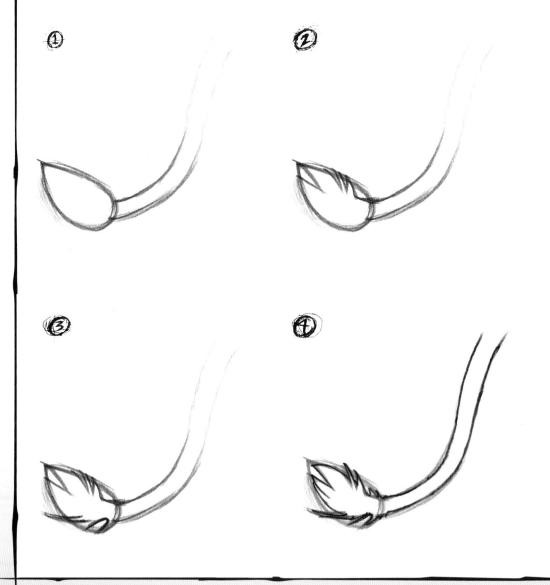

Lion ②

The story of Samson is one of my favorites in the Bible. My favorite part is when he's suddenly attacked by a lion in the vineyard. The Bible says that he tore the lion in two with his bare hands! That could only be strength from God. Imagine this lion coming at you in the wilderness when you are all alone. Scary thought...but apparently not to Samson!

Step ①

These circles form the framework for the head and body. Try to keep the sizes and positions in perspective.

 # Step ②

We're going to use some odd shapes to build the head and legs. These steps may seem strange now, but they will help us in the last few steps.

 # Step ③

The legs are nearly done. Don't worry about keeping your lines clean and neat because we're going to erase them soon.

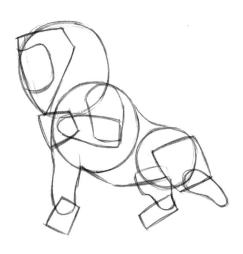

Step ④

Add the shapes for the ears, face, claws, and tail. I call all these shapes the foundation because they help us build the rest of the drawing.

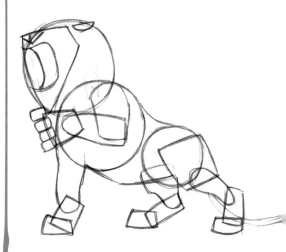

Step ⑤

Use your pen or dark pencil to outline the lion in detail. Take your time in places like the teeth and the mane. The more time you take while you're learning, the better artist you'll be.

Step ⑥

Here we've added a line to represent a closed eye. We also drew in the detail in the paws. Start erasing the rough pencil shapes.

Step ⑦

Add the lion's molar teeth, as well a few little bits of musculature in the paws and leg. We're almost done with this cat.

Step ⑧

And the last step is the claws. Congratulations on making it through that drawing. It wasn't an easy one. Practice makes you better!

teeth Detail

Yeah, so about those teeth... They're scary, but they are really fun to draw. Remember that it's very helpful for you to do these lessons more than once. The next time you draw the lion's head, flip to this page and follow these instructions.

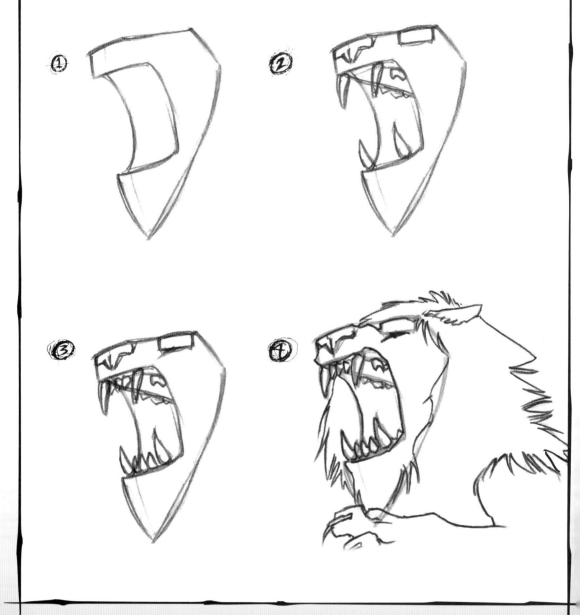

Serpent before the Fall

After Adam and Eve sinned in the garden of Eden, God cursed the earth. Man had to pay the price of sin by being separated from God. In Genesis 3, it was the serpent who deceived Adam and Eve with his craftiness. And as a result the serpent became cursed above all other creatures. He was cursed to crawl on his belly forever. The question I always ask is, how did the serpent get around before he slithered? Did he walk? Did he fly? Did he have wings or feet? If so, how many? We don't know, but for the sake of simplicity, let's draw a four-legged, pre-cursed snake.

Step ①

Here's the whole body of the snake, along with a portion of the head. Don't forget to keep your lines light and rough.

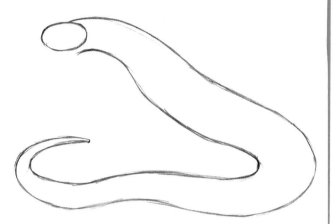

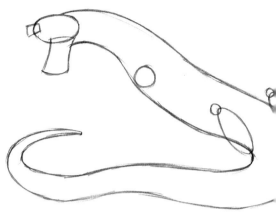 Step ②

We're slowly going to build onto the head as well as start the basic shapes of the legs.

Step ③

Now that head is taking shape! Just a couple more geometric shapes and we'll be ready to start on the outline.

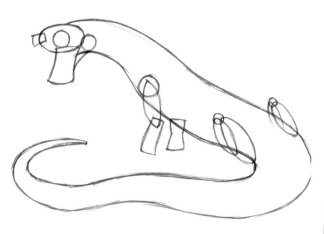

 Step ④

Notice that the feet aren't perfect squares; they're kind of oddly shaped. Now we're ready to switch to darker pencil or pen.

Step ⑤

Here comes the fun part—fangs! Try to make them sharp as needles. Also, take your time while you're doing the claws. Check out the detail section of these claws for more instruction.

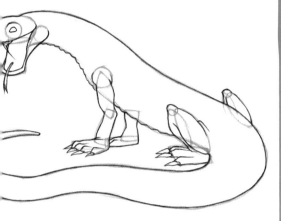

Step ⑥

Snakes have a lot of soft tissue in their mouth, so we need to add some lines in the there to make it appear lumpy and soft. We also need a nostril and a line behind the eye.

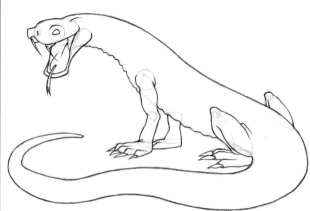

Step ⑦

Now we're adding a bunch of scales under the belly. Take your time. All those little lines take patience. Take a break if you need one.

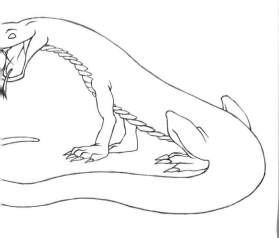

Step ⑧

Lastly, we draw the crest of the snake's back to show where it twists around in perspective. Remember, you can try it again. Practice makes you a better artist.

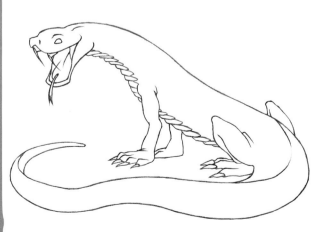

Foot Detail

Since no one has ever seen snake feet before, I figured I better give you a close-up on how to draw them. Since this creature is imaginary, you can make the feet look different if you want to. You could add fur, or spikes, or even longer claws. So remember to have fun because that's what drawing is all about!

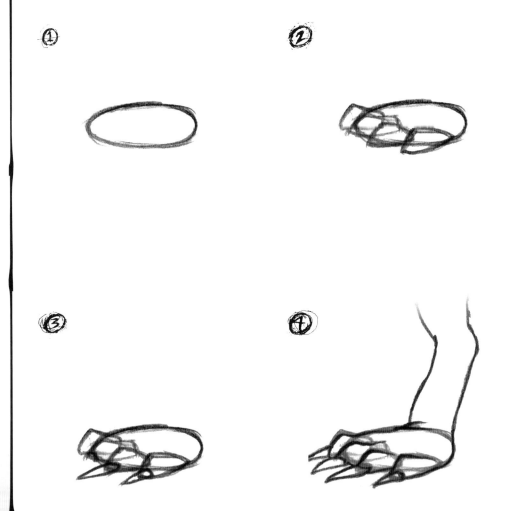

Bear

When King David was a young shepherd boy, he got into some serious fights. He was not fighting on the playground or with his brothers, but in the wilderness against lions and bears. Well, bears are fun to draw, and this will be good practice for drawing hair and fur. From a distance, bears often look very friendly, but check out this bear's teeth and claws! Imagine facing it alone with nothing but a walking stick and a sling!

Step ①

Here are some basic shapes for the head. Don't worry about the quality of your lines, because we'll be erasing them.

Step ②

Here is a bean shape for the body and a circle for the pelvis area.

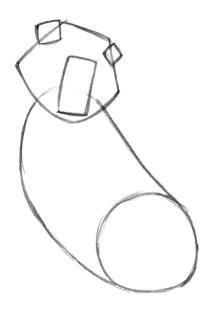

Step ③

Although these ovals seem odd now, they are the structural framework of the upper arm and lower leg of the bear.

Step ④

Here are the rest of the geometric shapes we need to build this bear.

Step 5

In this step, there's a lot of hair, fur, and claws. Take your time as you outline with pen. If you're having trouble with the claws, just skip ahead to the detail section of this lesson.

Step 6

All we're adding in this step is some definition in the snout to make the mouth.

Step 7

Finish the nose, eyes, and teeth. Remember that your drawing doesn't have to look exactly the same as mine.

Step 8

To finish this off, add a little more detail on the ears and eyebrows. Bears often have a lazy lower lip. Add those lines to show that this bear's lip is sagging a little. Congratulations, we're done!

Paw Details

Check out the detail lessons for the camel and the lion for help with the fur. Here are some details on the paw and claws of this bear. You're welcome to make them smaller or bigger if you want.

Camel

Three of the most common methods of travel in the Bible were by horse, donkey, and camel. Camels have some really crazy shapes. I think they're some of the most unique-looking animals out there. Look carefully at this image of the camel to help you understand all the little parts that seem insignificant.

Step ①

There are two circles here. One will become the hump of the camel, and the other will become the body.

Step ②

Two more circles and a neck will form the head and neck of the camel. There's also a little square that will become the ear.

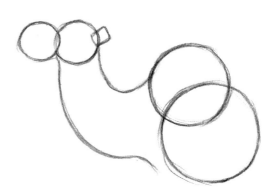

Step ③

These shapes that look like upside-down bowling pins will become the legs and knobby knees.

Step ④

It looks like a camel now, so we can start adding the pen detail and erasing some of the basic shapes.

Step 5

Now our camel is taking shape. Don't erase the geometric shapes completely, because you may need to see them for the next step. Remember the tail!

Step 6

These lines show that there are three blankets over the hump. There's also some new detail on the head.

Step 7

Add those tassels to the blanket on the hump. Also add big black eyes and a nostril. Those camels have big nostrils!

Step 8

Now we need the harness on the head. We also added knee pads because a camel kneels every time its rider gets on and off. There's also a little more hair detail in the neck. And we're done!

Hair and Fur Detail

I usually have a pretty good idea of what my drawing is going to look like before I draw it. The one part of the drawing I never really know about is the hair and fur. Hair and fur never look the same, so don't get discouraged. But, here are some guidelines I give myself to help me create convincing hair. And these camels have a lot of it!

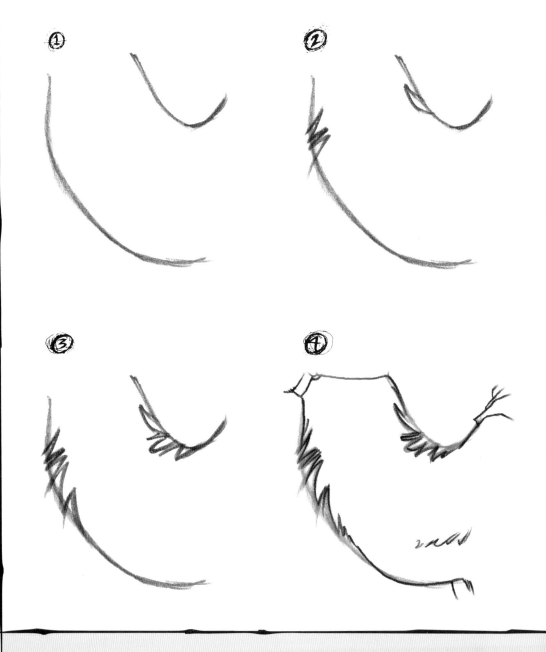

Locust

There are two major references to locusts in Bible. The first is the plague of locusts sent by God into Egypt. Imagine millions of this creature swarming over the land and devouring all of the crops that the farmers worked so hard to grow. It must have been devastating for Pharaoh to see...but that's what God wanted. God used these tiny little creatures to pressure Pharaoh into releasing the Israelites. The second reference to locusts is in Leviticus 11 when God refers to the locust as an insect that is okay for the Israelites to eat. Blechh!

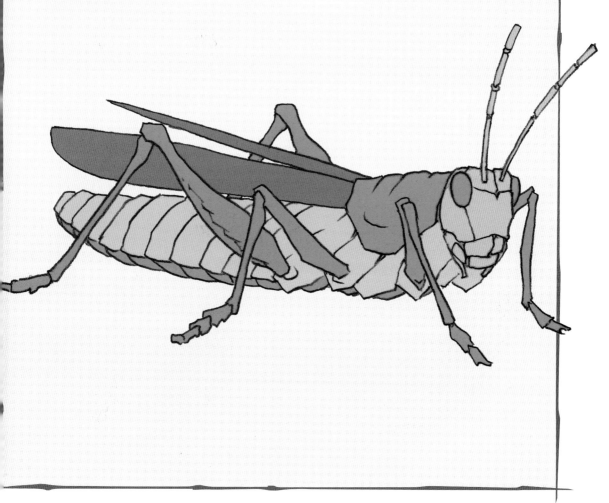

Step ①

Well this just looks like a banana with a head, doesn't it? It's going to be the head and body of the locust.

Step ②

Those upside-down bowling pins are going to serve as legs. Notice there are only four at this point. We're going to add the fifth later. Also, add the shell on the back. The sixth leg is hidden by the body of the locust. Remember to draw what you see instead of what you know.

Step ③

There's that fifth leg. We're also blocking out the wings. They are different shapes because they are at different angles.

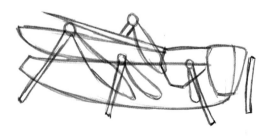

Step ④

Now the legs and antennae are blocked out and ready to draw.

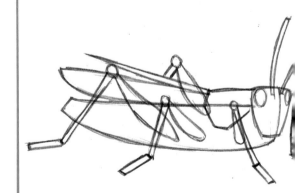

Step 5

Many parts of this locust are segmented, including the antennae. The head also has a lot of sections. For more help with these, skip ahead to the detail page.

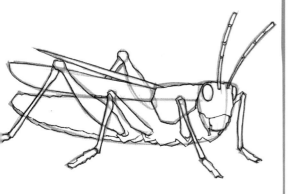

 Step 6

The abdomen is also segmented, so we should add those segments in this step. You don't have to have the same number of segments as pictured here.

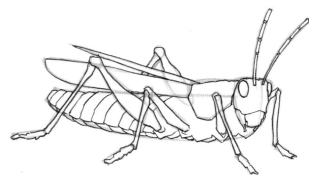

Step 7

We need to break up the thorax into noticeable sections as well.

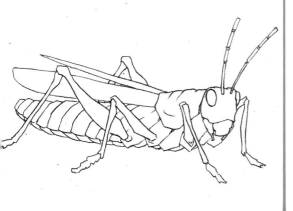

Step 8

And finally, you can break up the ends of the feet and the head into sections. If you used a pen you can erase the remainder of the foundation shapes.

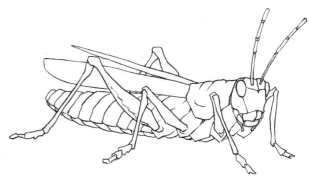

Head Detail

The hardest part of this drawing for me was figuring out how these little pieces of the head all fit together. So just follow these steps to block out those shapes, and maybe with a little practice we'll be able to recreate a perfect locust head.

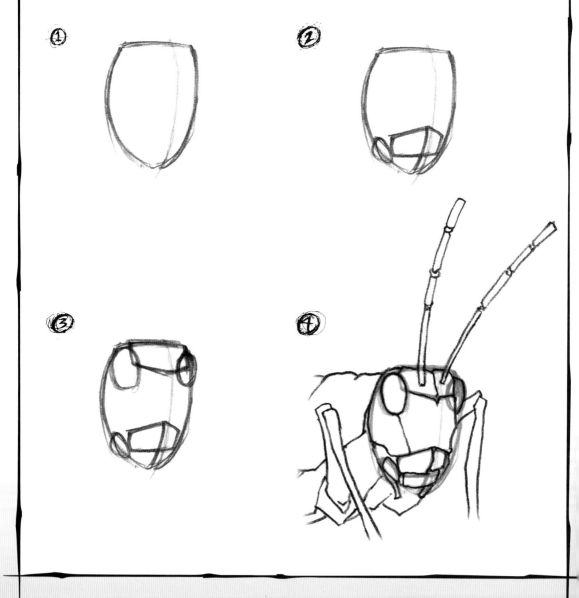

Behemoth

Does this beast look like anything you've seen at the zoo lately? In Job 40, Job describes one of the greatest creatures that God created. There's lots of debate as to whether Job is describing a hippopotamus, an elephant, a dinosaur, or a beast that no one has ever seen or heard of. Job just simply calls it a behemoth. Let's learn how to draw my personal interpretation of the behemoth.

Step ①

Here are three easy circles. Remember to press lightly; these are just the building blocks of the drawing.

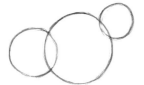

Step ②

You're welcome to make the tail or neck longer or shorter if you want since no one has seen this animal before.

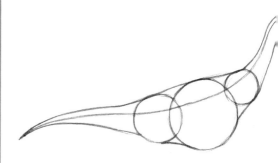

Step ③

These ovals are the starting shapes for the legs. We're going to work down from here to build powerful legs.

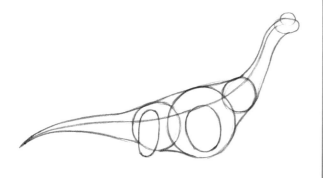

Step ④

Now there are only three legs visible here. It's because we're going to add the fourth leg in the next step when we go to pen.

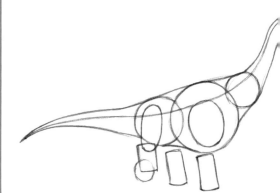

Step ⑤

Notice how the front leg is kind of hidden behind the other? Try to keep all those bumps and curves in the lines for all the wrinkles we'll add later on. Look at the final drawing as a guide.

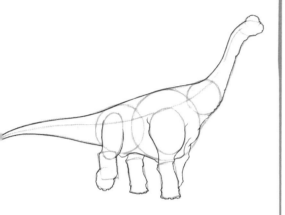

Step ⑥

Let's add some of those wrinkles, and toes to the legs. Also add a dot for the eye.

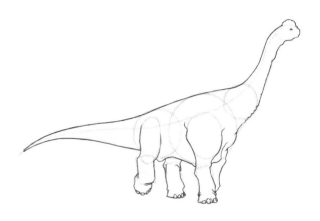

Step ⑦

Add more wrinkles—like an elephant—to the belly and leg. Add the final detail to the head.

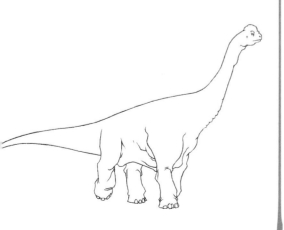

Step ⑧

Well the behemoth is done, but you can add those birds up there to show scale, meaning how large this beast is compared to another animal. Good job!

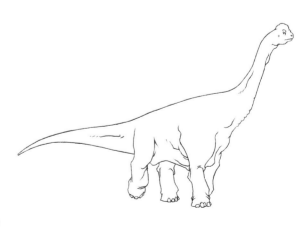

Leg Detail

Like I said, this is just my version of Job's behemoth. If I had to draw it again, maybe I'd draw it differently. If you want, you can draw your own version and email it to me so I can learn how to draw your version of the behemoth. Here's some instruction on getting those legs to look more like rods of iron as Job described.

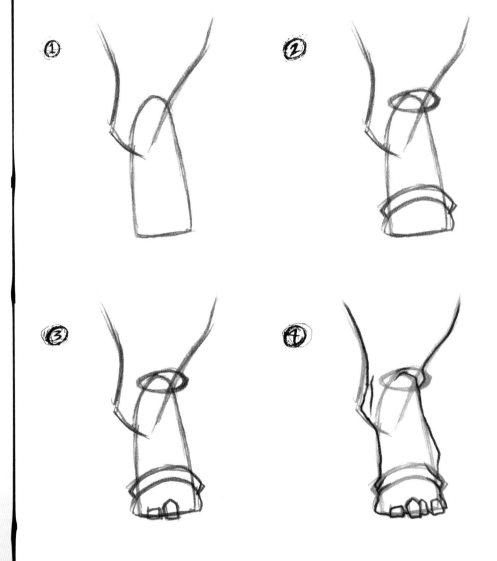

Leviathan

What on earth is Job describing? That's what a lot of people ask when they read Job 41. The chapter describes a terrible monster from the deeps of the ocean: scales as big as shields; rows of teeth inside the mouth; and "firebrands" leaping from its nostrils. Some scholars say that he's talking about a crocodile, but others believe that he's talking about an amazing creature long extinct. The truth is we'll never know for sure in this lifetime. But it's still one of my favorite chapters in the Old Testament.

Step ①

Let's start with the body and head. If you've got more space on your page than I did, you're welcome to make the tail longer.

Step ②

We're building the structure beneath the head here, as well as the front arms and back fins.

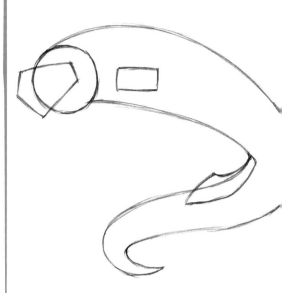

Step ③

Add more shapes around the head that we'll use to build the jaw. Also the little arms at the front are beginning to take shape.

Step ④

You're ready to draw the head. If you'd like a more detailed breakdown of the eyes and brow and teeth, skip ahead to the detail section.

Add the teeth and detail on the arms and fins. Look to the final drawing to understand why you're adding bumps and twists here.

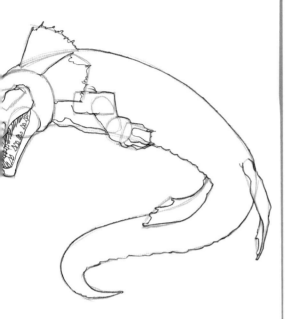

We're now adding all the little spines to those fins around the head and tail. And don't forget the eyes and face detail.

We need to add that armored underbelly. Take your time with these lines. They don't have to look exactly the same; they just have to look close.

And finally, add a row of shields along the back. Maybe Job meant bony spines like this. Add the skin details to finish.

Head Detail

Well that was a fantastic creature we drew. For this detail section, I'm simply going to break down the head into slightly more complex shapes than we did the first time. If you had a hard time with that lumpy head, then just follow these few instructions.

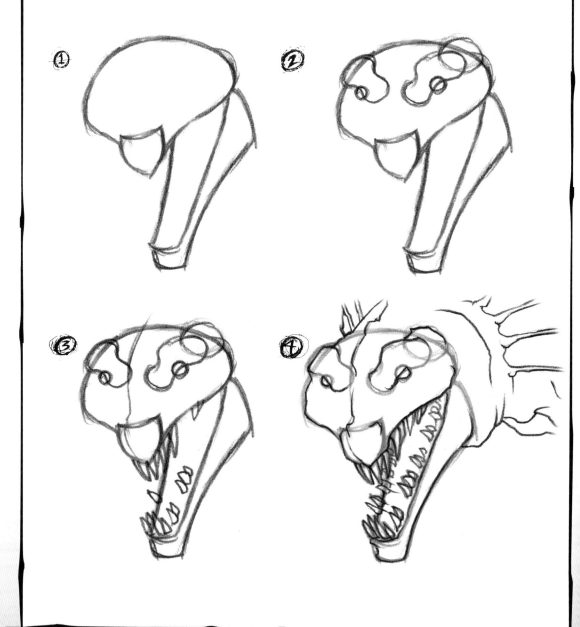

DEVOTIONS TO MAKE YOU STRONGER

Devotions to Make You Stronger is a 90-day devotional book written specifically for boys ages 8-12. Its relevant messages are written in the humorous, gross style of the 2:52 Boy's Bible and the 2:52 books, and are designed to ignite the interest of reluctant readers. Each reading begins with a Bible verse, followed by an explanation and a paragraph relating the lesson to today's boys. The boys are then given tools to help them cope and inspire them to change their lives.

Softcover 0-310-71311-0

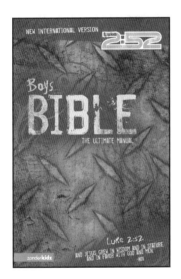

THE 2:52 BOYS BIBLE (NIV)

Using the example of Jesus from Luke 2:52 as its guide, The NIV 252 Bible shows boys ages 8-12 how to be deeper, stronger, smarter, and cooler.

Hardcover 0-310-70320-4 • Softcover 0-310-70552-5

NIV 2:52 NIV BACKPACK BIBLE

The full NIV text in a handy size for boys on the go—for ages 8 and up.

Italian Duo-Tone™ Brown/Orange 0-310-71417-6

BIG BAD
BIBLE
GIANTS

Softcover
0-310-70869-9

CREEPY
CREATURES
& BIZARRE
BEASTS FRo
THE BIBLE

Softcover
0-310-70654-8

BIBLE
ANGELS
& DEMONS

Softcover
0-310-70775-7

WEIRD &
GROSS
BIBLE
STUFF

Softcover
0-310-70484-7

BIBLE
HEROES &
BAD GUYS

Softcover
0-310-70322-0

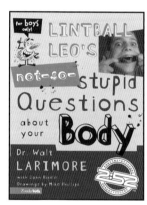

LINTBALL
LEo's NOT-
so-STUPID
QUESTIONS
ABOUT
YOUR BODY

Softcover
0-310-70545-2

BIBLE
WARS &
WEAPONS

Softcover
0-310-70323-9

THE BOOK
of COOL

Softcover
0-310-70696-3